The Nurnberg Stove

Ouida

The Nurnberg Stove

Table of Contents

The Nurnberg Stove 1
   Ouida 1
   I. 1
   II. 3
   III. 7
   IV. 10
   V. 16
   VI. 21
   VII. 24
   VIII. 26
   IX. 30
   X. 37
   XI. 40

The Nurnberg Stove

Ouida

Kessinger Publishing reprints thousands of hard-to-find books!

Visit us at http://www.kessinger.net

- I
- II
- III
- IV
- V
- VI
- VII
- VIII
- IX
- X
- XI

I

AUGUST lived in a little town called Hall. Hall is a favorite name for several towns in Austria and in Germany, but this one especial little Hall, in the Upper Innthal, is one of the most charming Old-World places that I know, and August for his part did not know any other. It has the green meadows and the great mountains all about it, and the gray-green glacier-fed water rushes by it. It has paved, streets and enchanting little shops that have all latticed panes and iron gratings to them; it has a very grand old Gothic church, that has the noblest blendings of light and shadow, and marble tombs of dead knights, and a look of infinite strength and repose as a church should have. Then there is

The Nurnberg Stove

the Muntze Tower, black and white, rising out of greenery and looking down on a long wooden bridge and the broad rapid river; and there is an old schloss which has been made into a guardhouse, with battlements and frescos and heraldic devices in gold and colors, and a man-at-arms carved in stone standing life-size in his niche and, bearing his date 1580. A little farther on, but close at hand, is a cloister with beautiful marble columns and tombs, and a colossal wood-carved Calvary, and beside that a small and very rich chapel: indeed, so full is the little town of the undisturbed past, that to walk in it is like opening a missal of the Middle Ages, all emblazoned and illuminated with saints and warriors, and it is so clean, and so still, and so noble, by reason of its monuments and its historic color, that I marvel much no one has ever cared to sing its praises. The old pious heroic life of an age at once more restful and more brave than ours still leaves its spirit there, and then there is the girdle of the mountains all around, and that alone means strength, peace, majesty.

In this little town a few years ago August Strehla lived with his people in the stone-paved irregular square where the grand church stands.

He was a small boy of nine years at that time,—a chubby-faced little man with rosy cheeks, big hazel eyes, and clusters of curls the brown of ripe nuts. His mother was dead, his father was poor, and there were many mouths at home to feed. In this country the winters are long and very cold, the whole land lies wrapped in snow for many months, and this night that he was trotting home, with a jug of beer in his numb red hands, was terribly cold and dreary. The good burghers of Hall had shut their double shutters, and the few lamps there were flickered dully behind their quaint, old-fashioned iron casings. The mountains indeed were beautiful, all snow-white under the stars that are so big in frost. Hardly any one was astir; a few good souls wending home from vespers, a tired postboy who blew a shrill blast from his tasselled horn as he pulled up his sledge before a hostelry, and little August hugging his jug of beer to his ragged sheepskin coat, were all who were abroad, for the snow fell heavily and the good folks of Hall go early to their beds. He could not run, or he would have spilled the beer; he was half frozen and a little frightened, but he kept up his courage by saying over and over again to himself, "I shall soon be at home with dear Hirschvogel."

He went on through the streets, past the stone man-at-arms of the guard house, and so into the place where the great church was, and where near it stood his father, Karl Strehla's house, with a sculptured Bethlehem over the door-way, and the Pilgrimage of

The Nurnberg Stove

the Three Kings painted on its wall. He had been sent on a long errand outside the gates in the afternoon, over the frozen fields and the broad white snow, and had been belated, and had thought he had heard the wolves behind him at every step, and had reached the town in a great state of terror, thankful with all his little panting heart to see the oil-lamp burning under the first house-shrine. But he had not forgotten to call for the beer, and he carried it carefully now, though his hands were so numb that he was afraid they would let the jug down every moment.

The snow outlined with white every gable and cornice of the beautiful old wooden houses; the moonlight shone on the gilded signs, the lambs, the grapes, the eagles, and all the quaint devices that hung before the doors; covered lamps burned before the Nativities and Crucifixions painted on the walls or let into the wood-work; here and there, where a shutter had not been closed, a ruddy fire-light lit up a homely interior, with the noisy band of children clustering round the housemother and a big brown loaf, or some gossips spinning and listening to the cobbler's or the barber's story of a neighbor, while the oil-wicks glimmered, and the hearth-logs blazed, and the chestnuts sputtered in their iron roasting-pot. Little August saw all these things, as he saw everything with his two big bright eyes that had such curious lights and shadows in them; but he went heedfully on his way for the sake of the beer which a single slip of the foot would make him spill. At his knock and call the solid oak door, four centuries old if one, flew open, and the boy darted in with his beer, and shouted, with all the force of mirthful lungs, "Oh, dear Hirschvogel, but for the thought of you I should have died!"

It was a large barren room into which he rushed with so much pleasure, and the bricks were bare and uneven. It had a walnut-wood press, handsome and very old, a broad deal table, and several wooden stools for all its furniture; but at the top of the chamber, sending out warmth and color together as the lamp shed its rays upon it, was a tower of porcelain, burnished with all the hues of a king's peacock and a queen's jewels, and surmounted with armed figures, and shields, and flowers of heraldry, and a great golden crown upon the highest summit of all.

II

IT was a stove of 1532, and on it were the letters H. R. H., for it was in every portion the handwork of the great potter of Nurnberg, Augustin Hirschvogel, who put his mark thus,

The Nurnberg Stove

as all the world knows.

The stove no doubt had stood in palaces and been made for princes, had warmed the crimson stockings of cardinals and the gold-broidered shoes of archduchesses, had glowed in presence-chambers and lent its carbon to help kindle sharp brains in anxious councils of state; no one knew what it had seen or done or been fashioned for; but it was a right royal thing. Yet perhaps it had never been more useful than it was now in this poor desolate room, sending down heat and comfort into the troop of children tumbled together on a wolf-skin at its feet, who received frozen August among them with loud shouts of joy.

"Oh, dear Hirschvogel, I am so cold, so cold!" said August, kissing its gilded lion's claws, "Is father not in, Dorothea?"

"No, dear. He is late."

Dorothea was a girl of seventeen, dark-haired and serious, and with a sweet sad face, for she had had many cares laid on her shoulders, even whilst still a mere baby. She was the eldest of the Strehla family, and there were ten of them in all. Next to her there came Jan and Karl and Otho, big lads, gaining a little for their own living; and then came August, who went up in the summer to the high Alps with the farmers' cattle, but in winter could do nothing to fill his own little platter and pot; and then all the little ones, who could only open their mouths to be fed like young birds,—Albrecht and Hilda, and Waldo and Christof, and last of all little three-year-old Ermengilda, with eyes like forget-me-nots, whose birth had cost them the life of their mother.

They were of that mixed race, half Austrian, half Italian, so common in the Tyrol; some of the children were white and golden as lilies, others were brown and brilliant as fresh-fallen chestnuts. The father was a good man, but weak and weary with so many to find for and so little to do it with. He worked at the salt-furnaces, and by that gained a few florins; people said he would have worked better and kept his family more easily if he had not loved his pipe and a draught of ale too well; but this had only been said of him after his wife's death, when trouble and perplexity had begun to dull a brain never too vigorous, and to enfeeble further a character already too yielding. As it was, the wolf often bayed at the door of the Strehla household, without a wolf from the mountains coming down. Dorothea was one of those maidens who almost work miracles, so far can

The Nurnberg Stove

their industry and care and intelligence make a home sweet and wholesome and a single loaf seem to swell into twenty. The children were always clean and happy, and the table was seldom without its big pot of soup once a day. Still, very poor they were, and Dorothea's heart ached with shame, for she knew that their father's debts were many for flour and meat and clothing. Of fuel to feed the big stove they had always enough without cost, for their mother's father was alive, and sold wood and fir cones and coke, and never grudged them to his grandchildren, though he grumbled at Strehla's improvidence and hapless, dreamy ways.

"Father says we are never to wait for him: we will have supper, now you have come home, dear," said Dorothea, who, however she might fret her soul in secret as she knitted their hose and mended their shirts, never let her anxieties cast a gloom on the children; only to August she did speak a little sometimes, because he was so thoughtful and so tender of her always, and knew, as well as she did that there were troubles about money,—though these troubles were vague to them both, and the debtors were patient and kindly, being neighbors all in the old twisting streets between the guard-house and the river.

Supper was a huge bowl of soup, with big slices of brown bread swimming in it and some onions bobbing up and down: the bowl was soon emptied by ten wooden spoons, and then the three eldest boys slipped off to bed, being tired with their rough bodily labor in the snow all day, and Dorothea drew her spinning-wheel by the stove and set it whirring, and the little ones got August down upon the old worn wolf-skin and clamored to him for a picture or a story. For August was the artist of the family.

He had a piece of planed deal that his father had given him, and some sticks of charcoal, and he would draw a hundred things he had seen in the day, sweeping each out with his elbow when the children had seen enough of it and sketching another in its stead,—faces and dogs' heads, and men in sledges, and old women in their furs, and pine-trees, and cocks and hens, and all sorts of animals, and now and then—very reverently—a Madonna and Child. It was all very rough, for there was no one to teach him anything. But it was all life-like, and kept the whole troop of children shrieking with laughter, or watching breathless, with wide open, wondering, awed eyes.

They were all so happy: what did they care for the snow outside? Their little bodies were warm, and their hearts merry; even Dorothea, troubled about the bread for the morrow,

The Nurnberg Stove

laughed as she spun; and August, with all his soul in his work, and little rosy Ermengilda's cheek on his shoulder, glowing after his frozen afternoon, cried out loud, smiling, as he looked up at the stove that was shedding its heat down on them all,—

"Oh, dear Hirschvogel! you are almost as great and good as the sun! No; you are greater and better, I think, because he goes away nobody knows where all these long, dark, cold hours, and does not care how people die for want of him; but you—you are always ready: just a little bit of wood to feed you, and you will make a summer for us all the winter through!"

The grand old stove seemed to smile through all its iridescent surface at the praises of the child. No doubt the stove, though it had known three centuries and more, had known but very little gratitude.

It was one of those magnificent stoves in enamelled faience which so excited the jealousy of the other potters of Nurnberg that in a body they demanded of the magistracy that Augustin Hirschvogel should be forbidden to make any more of them,—the magistracy, happily, proving of a broader mind, and having no sympathy with the wish of the artisans to cripple their greater fellow.

It was of great height and breadth, with all the majolica lustre which Hirschvogel learned to give to his enamels when he was making love to the young Venetian girl whom he afterwards married. There was the statue of a king at each corner, modelled with as much force and splendor as his friend Albrecht Durer could have given unto them on copperplate or canvas. The body of the stove itself was divided into panels, which had the Ages of Man painted on them in polychrome; the borders of the panels had roses and holly and laurel and other foliage, and German mottoes in black letter of odd Old–World moralizing, such as the old Teutons, and the Dutch after them, love to have on their chimney–places and their drinking–cups, their dishes and flagons. The whole was burnished with gilding in many parts, and was radiant everywhere with that brilliant coloring of which the Hirschvogel family, painters on glass and great in chemistry, as they were, were all masters.

The stove was a very grand thing, as I say: possibly Hirschvogel had made it for some mighty lord of the Tyrol at that time when he was an imperial guest at Innspruck and fashioned so many things for the Schloss Amras and beautiful Philippine Welser, the burgher's daughter, who gained an archduke's heart by her beauty and the right to wear his honors by her wit. Nothing was known of the stove at this latter day in Hall. The grandfather Strehla, who had been a master-mason, had dug it up out of some ruins where he was building, and, finding it without a flaw, had taken it home, and only thought it worth finding because it was such a good one to burn. That was now sixty years past, and ever since then the stove had stood in the big desolate empty room, warming three generations of the Strehla family, and having seen nothing prettier perhaps in all its many years than the children tumbled now in a cluster like gathered flowers at its feet. For the Strehla children, born to nothing else, were all born with beauty: white or brown, they were equally lovely to look upon, and when they went into the church to mass, with their curling locks and their clasped hands, they stood under the grim statues like cherubs flown down off some fresco.

III

"Tell us a story, August," they cried, in chorus, when they had seen charcoal pictures till they were tired; and August did as he did every night pretty nearly, looked up at the stove and told them what he imagined of the many adventures and joys and sorrows of the human being who figured on the panels from his cradle to his grave.

To the children the stove was a household god. In summer they laid a mat of fresh moss all round it, and dressed it up with green boughs and the numberless beautiful wild flowers of the Tyrol country. In winter all their joys centred in it, and scampering home from school over the ice and snow they were happy, knowing that they would soon be cracking nuts or roasting chestnuts in the broad ardent glow of its noble tower, which rose eight feet high above them with all its spires and pinnacles and crowns.

Once a travelling peddler had told them that the letters on it meant Augustin Hirschvogel, and that Hirschvogel had been a great German potter and painter, like his father before him, in the art-sanctified city of Nurnberg, and had made many such stoves, that were all miracles of beauty and of workmanship, putting all his heart and his soul and his faith into his labors, as the men of those earlier ages did, and thinking but little of gold or praise.

An old trader, too, who sold curiosities not far from the church had told August a little

The Nurnberg Stove

more about the brave family of Hirschvogel, whose houses can be seen in Nurnberg to this day; of old Veit, the first of them, who painted the Gothic windows of St. Sebald with the marriage of the Margravine; of his sons and of his grandsons, potters, painters, engravers all, and chief of them great Augustin, the Luca della Robbia of the North. And August's imagination, always quick, had made a living personage out of these few records, and saw Hirschvogel as though he were in the flesh walking up and down the Maximilian-Strass in his visit to Innspruck, and maturing beautiful things in his brain as he stood on the bridge and gazed on the emerald-green flood of the Inn.

So the stove had got to be called Hirschvogel in the family, as if it were a living creature, and little August was very proud because he had been named after that famous old dead German who had had the genius to make so glorious a thing. The children loved the stove, but with August the love of it was a passion; and in his secret heart he used to say to himself, "When I am a man, I will make just such things too, and then I will set Hirschvogel in a beautiful room in a house that I will build myself in Innspruck just outside the gates, where the chestnuts are, by the river: that is what I will do when I am a man."

For August, a salt-baker's son and a little cow-keeper when he was anything, was a dreamer of dreams, and when he was upon the high Alps with his cattle, with the stillness and the sky around him, was quite certain that he would live for greater things than driving the herds up when the spring-tide came among the blue sea of gentians, or toiling down in the town with wood and with timber as his father and grandfather did every day of their lives. He was a strong and healthy little fellow, fed on the free mountain-air, and he was very happy, and loved his family devotedly, and was as active as a squirrel and as playful as a hare; but he kept his thoughts to himself, and some of them went a very long way for a little boy who was only one among many, and to whom nobody had ever paid any attention except to teach him his letters and tell him to fear God. August in winter was only a little, hungry school-boy, trotting to be catechised by the priest, or to bring the loaves from the bake-house, or to carry his father's boots to the cobbler; and in summer he was only one of hundreds of cow-boys, who drove the poor, half-blind, blinking, stumbling cattle, ringing their throat-bells, out into the sweet intoxication of the sudden sunlight, and lived up with them in the heights among the Alpine roses, with only the clouds and the snow-summits near. But he was always thinking, thinking, thinking, for all that; and under his little sheepskin winter coat and, his rough hempen summer shirt his heart had as much courage in it as Hofer's ever had,—great Hofer, who is a household

The Nurnberg Stove

word in all the Inl, and whom August always reverently remembered when he went to the city of Innspruck and ran out by the foaming water-mill and under the wooded height of Berg Isel.

August lay now in the warmth of the stove and told the children stories, his own little brown face growing red with excitement as his imagination glowed to fever-heat. That human being on the panels, who was drawn there as a baby in a cradle, as a boy playing among flowers, as a lover, sighing under a casement, as a soldier in the midst of strife, as a father with children round him, as a weary, old, blind man on crutches, and, lastly, as a ransomed soul raised up by angels, had always had the most intense interest for August, and he had made, not one history for him, but a thousand; he seldom told them the same tale twice. He had never seen a story-book in his life; his primer and his mass-book were all the volumes he had. But nature had given him Fancy, and she is a good fairy that makes up for the want of very many things! only, alas! her wings are so very soon broken, poor thing, and then she is of no use at all.

"It is time for you all to go to bed, children," said Dorothea, looking up from her spinning. "Father is very late to-night; you must not sit up for him."

"Oh, five minutes more, dear Dorothea!" they pleaded; and little rosy and golden Ermengilda climbed up into her lap. "Hirschvogel is so warm, the beds are never so warm as he. Cannot you tell us another tale, August?"

"No," cried August, whose face had lost its light, now that his story had come to an end, and who sat serious, with his hands clasped on his knees, gazing on to the luminous arabesques of the stove.

"It is only a week to Christmas," he said, suddenly.

"Grandmother's big cakes!" chuckled little Christof, who was five years old, and thought Christmas meant a big cake and nothing else.

"What will Santa Claus find for 'Gilda if she be good?" murmured Dorothea over the child's sunny head; for, however hard poverty might pinch, it could never pinch so tightly that Dorothea would not find some wooden toy and some rosy apples to put in her little sister's socks.

The Nurnberg Stove

"Father Max has promised me a big goose, because I saved the calf's life in June," said August; it was the twentieth time he had told them so that month, he was so proud of it.

"And Aunt Maila will be sure to send us wine and honey and a barrel of flour; she always does," said Albrecht. Their aunt Maila had a chalet and a little farm over on the green slopes towards Dorp Ampas.

"I shall go up into the woods and get Hirschvogel's crown," said August; they always crowned Hirschvogel for Christmas with pine boughs and ivy and mountain-berries. The heat soon withered the crown; but it was part of the religion of the day to them, as much so as it was to cross themselves in church and raise their voices in the "0 Salutaris Hostia."

And they fell chatting of all they would do on the Christ-night, and one little voice piped loud against another's, and they were as happy as though their stockings would be full of golden purses and jewelled toys, and the big goose in the soup-pot seemed to them such a meal as kings would envy,

IV

IN the midst of their chatter and laughter a blast of frozen air and a spray of driven snow struck like ice through the room, and reached them even in the warmth of the old wolf-skins and the great stove. It was the door which had opened and let in the cold; it was their father who had come home.

The younger children ran joyous to meet him. Dorothea pushed the one wooden arm-chair of the room to the stove, and August flew to set the jug of beer on a little round table, and fill a long clay pipe; for their father was good to them all, and seldom raised his voice in anger, and they had been trained by the mother they had loved to dutifulness and obedience and a watchful affection.

To-night Karl Strehla responded very wearily to the young ones' welcome, and came to the wooden chair with a tired step and sat down heavily, not noticing either pipe or beer.

"Are you not well, dear father?" his daughter asked him.

The Nurnberg Stove

"I am well enough," he answered, dully, and sat there with his head bent, letting the lighted pipe grow cold.

He was a fair, tall man, gray before his time, and bowed with labor.

"Take the children to bed," he said, suddenly, at last, and Dorothea obeyed. August stayed behind, curled before the stove; at nine years old, and when one earns money in the summer from the farmers, one is not altogether a child any more, at least in one's own estimation.

August did not heed his father's silence: he was used to it. Karl Strehla was a man of few words, and, being of weakly health, was usually too tired at the end of the day to do more than drink his beer and sleep. August lay on the wolf-skin, dreamy and comfortable, looking up through his drooping eyelids at the golden coronets on the crest of the great stove, and wondering for the millionth time whom it had been made for, and what grand places and scenes it had known.

Dorothea came down from putting the little ones in their beds; the cuckoo-clock in the corner struck eight; she looked to her father and the untouched pipe, then sat down to her spinning, saying nothing. She thought he had been drinking in some tavern; it had been often so with him of late.

There was a long silence; the cuckoo called the quarter twice; August dropped asleep, his curls falling over his face; Dorothea's wheel hummed like a cat.

Suddenly Karl Strehla struck his hand on the table, sending the pipe on the ground.

"I have sold Hirschvogel," he said; and his voice was husky and ashamed in his throat. The spinning-wheel stopped. August sprang erect out of his sleep.

"Sold Hirschvogel!" If their father had dashed the holy crucifix on the floor at their feet and spat on it, they could not have shuddered under the horror of a greater blasphemy.

"I have sold Hirschvogel!" said Karl Strehla, in the same husky, dogged voice. "I have sold it to a travelling trader in such things for two hundred florins. What would you?—I owe double that. He saw it this morning when you were all out. He will pack it and take it

The Nurnberg Stove

to Munich tomorrow."

Dorothea gave a low shrill cry.

"Oh, father!—the children—in mid-winter?"

She turned white as the snow without; her words died away in her throat.

August stood, half blind with sleep, staring with dazed eyes as his cattle stared at the sun when they came out from their winter's prison.

"It is not true! It is not true!" he muttered. "You are jesting, father?"

Strehla broke into a dreary laugh.

" It is true. Would you like to know what is true too?—that the bread you eat, and the meat you put in this pot, and the roof you have over your heads, are none of them paid for, have been none of them paid for for months and months: if it had not been for your grandfather I should have been in prison all summer and autumn, and he is out of patience and will do no more now. There is no work to be had; the masters go to younger men: they say I work ill; it may be so. Who can keep his head above water with ten hungry children dragging him down? When your mother lived, it was different. Boy, you stare at me as if I were a mad dog! You have made a god of yon china thing. Well—it goes: goes to-morrow. Two hundred florins, that is something. It will keep me out of prison for a little, and with the spring things may turn

August stood like a creature paralyzed. His eyes were wide open, fastened on his father's with terror and incredulous horror; his face had grown as white as his sister's; his chest heaved with tearless sobs.

"It is not true! It is not true!" he echoed, stupidly. It seemed to him that the very skies must fall, and the earth perish, if they could take away Hirschvogel. They might as soon talk of tearing down God's sun out of the heavens.

"You will find it true," said his father, doggedly, and angered because he was in his own soul bitterly ashamed to have bartered away the heirloom and treasure of his race and the

The Nurnberg Stove

comfort and health-giver of his young children. "You will find it true. The dealer has paid me half the money to-night, and will pay me the other half to-morrow when he packs it up and takes it away to Munich. No doubt it is worth a great deal more,—at least I suppose so, as he gives that,—but beggars cannot be choosers. The little black stove in the kitchen will warm you all just as well. Who would keep a gilded, painted thing in a poor house like this, when one can make two hundred florins by it? Dorothea, you never sobbed more when your mother died. What is it, when all is said?—a bit of hardware much too grand-looking for such a room as this. If all the Strehlas had not been born fools it would have been sold a century ago, when it was dug up out of the ground. 'It is a stove for a museum,' the trader said when he saw it. To a museum let it go."

August gave a shrill shriek like a hare's when it is caught for its death, and threw himself on his knees at his father's feet.

"Oh, father, father!" he cried, convulsively, his hands closing on Strehla's knees, and his uplifted face blanched and distorted with terror. "Oh, father, dear father, you cannot mean what you say? Send it away—our life, our sun, our joy; our comfort? We shall all die in the dark and cold. Sell me rather. Sell me to any trade or any pain you like; I will not mind. But Hirschvogel!—it is like selling the very cross off the altar! You must be in jest. You could not do such a thing—you could not!—you who have always been gentle and good, and who have sat in the warmth here year after year with our mother. It is not a piece of hardware, as you say; it is a living thing, for a great man's thoughts and fancies have put life into it, and it loves us though we are only poor little children, and we love it with all our hearts and souls, and up in heaven I am sure the dead Hirschvogel knows! Oh, listen; I will go and try and get work to-morrow! I will ask them to let me cut ice or make the paths through the snow. There must be something I could do, and I will beg the people we owe money to to wait; they are all neighbors, they will be patient. But sell Hirschvogel!—oh, never! never! never! Give the florins back to the vile man. Tell him it would be like selling the shroud out of mother's coffin, or the golden curls off Ermengilda's head! Oh, father, dear father! do hear me, for pity's sake!"

Strehla was moved by the boy's anguish. He loved his children, though he was often weary of them, and their pain was pain to him. But besides emotion, and stronger than emotion, was the anger that August roused in him: he hated and despised himself for the barter of the heirloom of his race, and every word of the child stung him with a stinging sense of shame.

The Nurnberg Stove

And he spoke in his wrath rather than in his sorrow.

"You are a little fool," he said, harshly, as they had never heard him speak. "You rave like a play-actor. Get up and go to bed. The stove is sold. There is no more to be said. Children like you have nothing to do with such matters. The stove is sold, and goes to Munich tomorrow. What is it to you? Be thankful I can get bread for you. Get on your legs, I say, and go to bed."

Strehla took up the jug of ale as he paused, and drained it slowly as a man who had no cares.

August sprang to his feet and threw his hair back off his face; the blood rushed into his cheeks, making them scarlet; his great soft eyes flamed alight with furious passion.

"You dare not!" he cried, aloud, "you dare not sell it, I say! It is not yours alone; it is ours—"

Strehla flung the emptied jug on the bricks with a force that shivered it to atoms, and, rising to his feet, struck his son a blow that felled him to the floor. It was the first time in all his life that he had ever raised his band against any one of his children.

Then he took the oil-lamp that stood at his elbow and stumbled off to his own chamber with a cloud before his eyes.

"What has happened?" said August, a little while later, as he opened his eyes and saw Dorothea weeping above him on the wolf-skin before the stove. He had been struck backward, and his head had fallen on the hard bricks where the wolf-skin did not reach. He sat up a moment, with his face bent upon his hands.

"I remember now," he said, very low, under his breath.

Dorothea showered kisses on him, while her tears fell like rain.

"But, oh, dear, how could you speak so to father?" she murmured. "It was very wrong."

The Nurnberg Stove

"No, I was right," said August, and his little mouth, that hitherto had only curled in laughter, curved downward with a fixed and bitter seriousness. "How dare he? How dare he?" he muttered, with his head sunk in his hands. "It is not his alone. It belongs to us all. It is as much yours and mine as it is his."

Dorothea could only sob in answer. She was too frightened to speak. The authority of their parents in the house had never in her remembrance been questioned.

"Are you hurt by the fall, dear August?" she murmured, at length, for he looked to her so pale and strange.

"Yes—no. I do not know. What does it matter?"

He sat up upon the wolf-skin with passionate pain upon his face; all his soul was in rebellion, and he was only a child and was powerless.

"It is a sin; it is a theft; it is an infamy," he said, slowly, his eyes fastened on the gilded feet of Hirschvogel.

"Oh, August, do not say such things of father!" sobbed his sister. "Whatever he does, we ought to think it right."

August laughed aloud.

"Is it right that he should spend his money in drink?—that he should let orders lie unexecuted—that he should do his work so ill that no one cares to employ him?—that he should live on grandfather's charity, and then dare sell a thing that is ours every whit as much as it is his? To sell Hirschvogel! Oh, dear God! I would sooner sell my soul!"

"August!" cried Dorothea, with piteous entreaty. He terrified her, she could not recognize her little, gay, gentle brother in those fierce and blasphemous words.

August laughed aloud again; then all at once his laughter broke down into bitterest weeping. He threw himself forward on the stove, covering it with kisses, and sobbing as though his heart would burst from his bosom.

The Nurnberg Stove

What could he do? Nothing, nothing, nothing!

"August, dear August," whispered Dorothea, piteously, and trembling all over,—for she was a very gentle girl, and fierce feeling terrified her,—"August, do not lie there. Come to bed: it is quite late. In the morning you will be calmer. It is horrible indeed, and we shall die of cold, at least the little ones; but if it be father's will—"

"Let me alone," said August, through his teeth, striving to still the storm of sobs that shook him from head to foot. "Let me alone. In the morning!—how can you speak of the morning?"

"Come to bed, dear," sighed his sister. "Oh, August, do not lie and look like that! you frighten me. Do come to bed."

"I shall stay here."

"Here! all night!"

"They might take it in the night. Besides, to leave it now!"

"But it is cold! the fire is out."

"It will never be warm any more, nor shall we."

All his childhood had gone out of him, all his gleeful, careless, sunny temper had gone with it; he spoke sullenly and wearily, choking down the great sobs in his chest. To him it was as if the end of the world had come.

His sister lingered by him while striving to persuade him to go to his place in the little crowded bedchamber with Albrecht and Waldo and Christof. But it was in vain. "I shall stay here," was all he answered her. And he stayed,—all the night long.

V

THE lamps went out; the rats came and ran across the floor; as the hours crept on through

The Nurnberg Stove

midnight and past, the cold intensified and the air of the room grew like ice. August did not move; he lay with his face downward on the golden and rainbow-hued pedestal of the household treasure, which henceforth was to be cold for evermore, an exiled thing in a foreign city in a far-off land.

Whilst yet it was dark his three elder brothers came down the stairs and let themselves out, each bearing his lantern and going to his work in stone-yard and timber-yard and at the salt-works. They did not notice him; they did not know what had happened.

A little later his sister came down with a light in her hand to make ready the house ere morning should break.

She stole up to him and laid her hand on his shoulder timidly.

"Dear August, you must be frozen. August, do look up! do speak!"

August raised his eyes with a wild, feverish, sullen look in them that she had never seen there. His face was ashen white: his lips were like fire. He had not slept all night; but his passionate sobs had given way to delirious waking dreams and numb senseless trances, which had alternated one on another all through the freezing, lonely, horrible hours.

"It will never be warm again," he muttered, "never again!"

Dorothea clasped him with trembling hands.

"August! do you not know me?" she cried, in an agony. "I am Dorothea. Wake up, dear—wake up! It is morning, only so dark!"

August shuddered all over.

"The morning!" he echoed.

He slowly rose up on to his feet.

"I will go to grandfather," he said, very low. "He is always good: perhaps he could save it."

The Nurnberg Stove

Loud blows with the heavy iron knocker of the house–door drowned his words. A strange voice called aloud through the keyhole,—

"Let me in! Quick!—there is no time to lose! More snow like this, and the roads will all be blocked. Let me in! Do you hear? I am come to take the great stove."

August sprang erect, his fists doubled, his eyes blazing.

"You shall never touch it!" he screamed; "you shall never touch it!"

"Who shall prevent us?" laughed a big man, who was a Bavarian, amused at the fierce little figure fronting him.

"I!" said August. "You shall never have it! you shall kill me first!"

"Strehla," said the big man, as August's father entered the room, "you have got a little mad dog here: muzzle him."

One way and another they did muzzle him. He fought like a little demon and hit out right and left, and one of his blows gave the Bavarian a black eye. But he was soon mastered by four grown men, and his father flung him with no light hand out from the door of the back entrance, and the buyers of the stately and beautiful stove set to work to pack it heedfully and carry it away;

When Dorothea stole out to look for August, he was nowhere in sight. She went back to little 'Gilda, who was ailing, and sobbed over the child, whilst the others stood looking on, dimly understanding that with Hirschvogel was going all the warmth of their bodies, all the light of their hearth.

Even their father now was sorry and ashamed; but two hundred florins seemed a big sum to him, and, after all, he thought the children could warm themselves quite as well at the black iron stove in the kitchen. Besides, whether he regretted it now or not, the work of the Nurnberg potter was sold irrevocably, and he had to stand still and see the men from Munich wrap it in manifold wrappings and bear it out; into the snowy air to where an ox–cart stood in waiting for it.

The Nurnberg Stove

In another moment Hirschvogel was gone,—gone forever and aye.

August had stood still for a time, leaning, sick and faint from the violence that had been used to him, against the back wall of the house. The wall looked on a court where a well was, and the backs of other houses, and beyond them the spire of the Mintze Tower and the peaks of the mountains.

Into the court an old neighbor hobbled for water, and, seeing the boy, said to him,—

"Child, is it true your father is selling the big painted stove?"

August nodded his head, then burst into a passion of tears.

"Well, for sure he is a fool," said the neighbor. "Heaven forgive me for calling him so before his own child! but the stove was worth a mint of money. I do remember in my young days, in old Anton's time (that was your great-grandfather, my lad), a stranger from Vienna saw it, and said that it was worth its weight in gold."

August's sobs went on their broken, impetuous course.

"I loved it! I loved it!" he moaned. "I do not care what its value was. I loved it! I loved it!"

"You little simpleton!" said the old man, kindly. "But you are wiser than your father, when all's said. If sell it he must, he should have taken it to good Herr Steiner over at Spruz, who would have given him honest value. But no doubt they took him over his beer,—ay, ay! but if I were you I would do better than cry. I would go after it."

August raised his head, the tears raining down his cheeks.

"Go after it when you are bigger," said the neighbor, with a good-natured wish to cheer him up a little. "The world is a small thing after all: I was a travelling clockmaker once upon a time, and I know that your stove will be safe enough whoever gets it; anything that can be sold for a round sum is always wrapped up in cotton wool by everybody. Ay, ay, don't cry so much; you will see your stove again some day,"

The Nurnberg Stove

Then the old man hobbled away to draw his brazen pail full of water at the well.

August remained leaning against the wall; his head was buzzing and his heart fluttering with the new idea which had presented itself to his mind. "Go after it," had said the old man. He thought, "Why not go with it?" He loved it better than any one, even better than Dorothea; and he shrank from the thought of meeting his father again, his father who had sold Hirschvogel.

He was by this time in that state of exaltation in which the impossible looks quite natural and commonplace. His tears were still wet on his pale cheeks, but they had ceased to fall. He ran out of the court-yard by a little gate, and across to the huge gothic porch of the church. From there he could watch unseen his father's house-door, at which were always hanging some blue-and-gray pitchers, such as are common and so picturesque in Austria, for a part of the house was let to a man who dealt in pottery.

He hid himself in the grand portico, which he had so often passed through to go to mass or compline within, and presently his heart gave a great leap, for he saw the straw-enwrapped stove brought out and laid with infinite care on the bullock-dray. Two of the Bavarian men mounted beside it, and the sleigh-wagon slowly crept over the snow of the place,—snow crisp and hard as stone. The noble old minster looked its grandest and most solemn, with its dark-gray stone and its vast archways, and its porch that was itself as big as many a church, and its strange gargoyles and lamp-irons black against the snow on its roof and on the pavement; but for once August had no eyes for it: he only watched for his old friend. Then he, a little unnoticeable figure enough, like a score of other boys in Hall, crept, unseen by any of his brothers or sisters, out of the porch and over the shelving uneven square, and followed in the wake of the dray.

Its course lay towards the station of the rail-way, which is close to the salt-works, whose smoke at times sullies this part of clean little Hall, though it does not do very much damage. From Hall the iron road runs northward through glorious country to Salzburg, Vienna, Prague, Buda, and southward over the Brenner into Italy. Was Hirschvogel going north or south? This at least he would soon know.

The Nurnberg Stove

VI

AUGUST had often hung about the little station, watching the trains come and go and dive into the heart of the hills and vanish. No one said anything to him for idling about; people are kind-hearted and easy of temper in this pleasant land, and children and dogs are both happy there. He heard the Bavarians arguing and vociferating a great deal, and learned that they meant to go too and wanted to go with the great stove itself. But this they could not do, for neither could the stove go by a passenger-train nor they themselves go in a goods-train. So at length they insured their precious burden for a large sum, and consented to send it by a luggage-train which was to pass through Hall in half an hour. The swift trains seldom deign to notice the existence of Hall at all. August heard, and a desperate resolve made itself up in his little mind. Where Hirschvogel went would he go. He gave one terrible thought to Dorothea—poor, gentle Dorothea!—sitting in the cold at home, then set to work to execute his project. How he managed it he never knew very clearly himself, but certain it is that when the goods-train from the north, that had come all the way from Linz on the Danube, moved out of Hall, August was hidden behind the stove in the great covered truck, and wedged, unseen and undreamt of by any human creature, amidst the cases of wood-carving, of clocks and clock-work, of Vienna toys, of Turkish carpets, of Russian skins, of Hungarian wines, which shared the same abode as did his swathed and bound Hirschvogel. No doubt he was very naughty, but it never occurred to him that he was so: his whole mind and soul were absorbed in the one entrancing idea, to follow his beloved friend and fire-king.

It was very dark in the closed truck, which had only a little window above the door; and it was crowded, and had a strong smell in it from the Russian hides and the hams that were in it. But August was not frightened; he was close to Hirschvogel, and presently he meant to be closer still; for he meant to do nothing less than get inside Hirschvogel itself. Being a shrewd little boy, and having had by great luck two silver groschen in his breeches-pocket, which he had earned the day before by chopping wood, be had bought some bread and sausage at the station of a woman there who knew him, and who thought he was going out to his uncle Joachim's chalet above Jenbach. This he had with him, and this he ate in the darkness and the lumbering, pounding, thundering noise which made him giddy, as never had he been in a train of any kind before. Still he ate, having had no breakfast, and being a child, and half a German, and not knowing at all how or when he ever would eat again.

The Nurnberg Stove

When he had eaten, not as much as he wanted, but as much as he thought was prudent (for who could say when he would be able to buy anything more?), he set to work like a little mouse to make a hole in the withes of straw and hay which enveloped the stove. If it had been put in a packing-case he would have been defeated at the onset. As it was, he gnawed, and nibbled, and pulled, and pushed, just as a mouse would have done, making his hole where he guessed that the opening of the stove was,—the opening through which he had so often thrust the big oak logs to feed it. No one disturbed him; the heavy train went lumbering on and on, and he saw nothing at all of the beautiful mountains, and shining waters, and great forests through which he was being carried. He was hard at work getting through the straw and hay and twisted ropes; and get through them at last he did, and found the door of the stove, which he knew so well, and which was quite large enough for a child of his age to slip through, and it was this which he had counted upon doing. Slip through he did, as he had often done at home for fun, and curled himself up there to see if he could anyhow remain during many hours. He found that he could; air came in through the brass fret-work of the stove; and with admirable caution in such a little fellow he leaned out, drew the hay and straw together, and rearranged the ropes, so that no one could ever have dreamed a little mouse had been at them. Then he curled himself up again, this time more like a dormouse than anything else; and, being safe inside his dear Hirschvogel and intensely cold, he went fast asleep as if he were in his own bed at home with Albrecht and Christof on either side of him. The train lumbered on, stopping often and long, as the habit of goods-trains is, sweeping the snow away with its cow-switcher, and rumbling through the deep heart of the mountains, with its lamps aglow like the eyes of a dog in a night of frost.

The train rolled on in its heavy, slow fashion, and the child slept soundly for a long while. When he did awake, it was quite dark outside in the land; he could not see, and of course he was in absolute darkness; and for a while he was sorely frightened, and trembled terribly, and sobbed in a quiet heart-broken fashion, thinking of them all at home. Poor Dorothea! how anxious she would be! How she would run over the town and walk up to grandfather's at Dorf Ampas, and perhaps even send over to Jenbach, thinking he had taken refuge with Uncle Joachim! His conscience smote him for the sorrow he must be even then causing to his gentle sister; but it never occurred to him to try and go back. If he once were to lose sight of Hirschvogel how could he ever hope to find it again? how could he ever know whither it had gone,—north, south, east, or west? The old neighbor had said that the world was small; but August knew at least that it must have a great many places in it: that he had seen himself on the maps on his schoolhouse walls. Almost

The Nurnberg Stove

any other little boy would, I think, have been frightened out of his wits at the position in which he found himself; but August was brave, and he had a firm belief that God and Hirschvogel would take care of him. The master-potter of Nurnberg was always present to his mind, a kindly; benign, and gracious spirit, dwelling manifestly in that porcelain tower whereof he had been the maker.

A droll fancy, you say? But every child with a soul in him has quite as quaint fancies as this one was of August's.

So he got over his terror and his sobbing both, though he was so utterly in the dark. He did not feel cramped at all, because the stove was so large, and air he had in plenty, as it came through the fret-work running round the top. He was hungry again, and again nibbled with prudence at his loaf and his sausage. He could not at all tell the hour. Every time the train stopped and he heard the banging, stamping, shouting, and jangling of chains that went on, his heart seemed to jump up into his mouth. If they should find him out! Sometimes porters came and took away this case and the other, a sack here, a bale there, now a big bag, now a dead chamois. Every time the men trampled near him, and swore at each other, and banged this and that to and fro, he was so frightened that his very breath seemed to stop. When they came to lift the stove out, would they find him? and if they did find him, would they kill him? That was what he kept thinking of all the way, all through the dark hours, which seemed without end. The goods-trains are usually very slow, and are many days doing what a quick train does in a few hours. This one was quicker than most, because it was bearing goods to the King of Bavaria; still, it took all the short winter's day and the long winter's night and half another day to go over ground that the mail-trains cover in a forenoon. It passed great armored Kuffstein standing across the beautiful and solemn gorge, denying the right of way to all the foes of Austria. It passed twelve hours later, after lying by in out-of-the-way stations, pretty Rosenheim, that marks the border of Bavaria. And here the Nurnberg stove, with August inside it, was lifted out heedfully and set under a covered way. When it was lifted out, the boy had hard work to keep in his screams; he was tossed to and fro as the men lifted the huge thing, and the earthenware walls of his beloved fire-king were not cushions of down. However, though they swore and grumbled at the weight of it, they never suspected that a living child was inside it, and they carried it out on to the platform and set it down under the roof of the goods-shed. There it passed the rest of the night and all the next morning, and August was all the while within it.

The Nurnberg Stove

VII

THE winds of early winter sweep bitterly ever Rosenheim, and all the vast Bavarian plain was one white sheet of snow. If there had not been whole armies of men at work always clearing the iron rails of the snow, no trains could ever have run at all. Happily for August, the thick wrappings in which the stove was enveloped and the stoutness of its own make screened him from the cold, of which, else, he must have died,—frozen. He had still some of his loaf, and a little—a very little—of his sausage. What he did begin to suffer from was thirst; and this frightened him almost more than anything else, for Dorothea had read aloud to them one night a story of the tortures some wrecked men had endured because they could not find any water but the salt sea. It was many hours since he had last taken a drink from the wooden spout of their old pump, which brought them the sparkling, ice-cold water of the hills.

But, fortunately for him, the stove, having been marked and registered as "fragile and valuable," was not treated quite like a mere bale of goods, and the Rosenheim station-master, who knew its consignees, resolved to send it on by a passenger-train that would leave there at daybreak. And when this train went out, in it, among piles of luggage belonging to other travellers, to Vienna, Prague, Buda-Pesth, Salzburg, was August, still undiscovered, still doubled up like a mole in the winter under the grass. Those words, "fragile and valuable," had made the men lift Hirschvogel gently and with care. He had begun to get used to his prison, and a little used to the incessant pounding and jumbling and rattling and shaking with which modern travel is always accompanied, though modern invention does deem itself so mightily clever. All in the dark he was, and he was terribly thirsty; but he kept feeling the earthenware sides of the Nurnberg giant and saying, softly, "Take care of me; oh, take care of me, dear Hirschvogel!"

He did not say, "Take me back;" for, now that he was fairly out in the world, he wished to see a little of it. He began to think that they must have been all over the world in all this time that the rolling and roaring and hissing and jangling had been about his ears; shut up in the dark, he began to remember all the tales that had been told in Yule round the fire at his grandfather's good house at Dorf, of gnomes and elves and subterranean terrors, and the Erl King riding on the black horse of night, and—and—and he began to sob and to tremble again, and this time did scream outright. But the steam was screaming itself so loudly that no one, had there been any one nigh, would have heard him; and in another

The Nurnberg Stove

minute or so the train stopped with a jar and a jerk, and he in his cage could hear men crying aloud, "Munchen! Munchen!"

Then he knew enough of geography to know that he was in the heart of Bavaria. He had had an uncle killed in the Bayerischenwald by the Bavarian forest guards, when in the excitement of hunting a black bear he had overpassed the limits of the Tyrol frontier.

That fate of his kinsman, a gallant young chamois–hunter who had taught him to handle a trigger and load a muzzle, made the very name of Bavaria a terror to August.

"It is Bavaria! It is Bavaria!" he sobbed to the stove; but the stove said nothing to him; it had no fire in it. A stove can no more speak without fire than a man can see without light. Give it fire, and it will sing to you, tell tales to you, offer you in return all the sympathy you ask.

"It is Bavaria!" sobbed August; for it is always a name of dread augury to the Tyroleans, by reason of those bitter struggles and midnight shots and untimely deaths which come from those meetings of jager and hunter in the Bayerischenwald. But the train stopped; Munich was reached, and August, hot and cold by turns, and shaking like a little aspen–leaf, felt himself once more carried out on the shoulders of men, rolled, along on a truck, and finally set down, where he knew not, only he knew he was thirsty,—so thirsty! If only he could have reached his hand out and scooped up a little snow!

He thought he had been moved on this truck many miles, but in truth the stove had been only taken from the railway–station to a shop in the Marienplatz. Fortunately, the stove was always set upright on its four gilded feet, an injunction to that effect having been affixed to its written label, and on its gilded feet it stood now in the small dark curiosity–shop of one Hans Rhilfer.

"I shall not unpack it till Anton comes," he heard a man's voice say; and then he heard a key grate in a lock, and by the unbroken stillness that ensued he concluded he was alone, and ventured to peep through the straw and hay. What he saw was a small square room filled with pots and pans, pictures, carvings, old blue jugs, old steel armor, shields, daggers, Chinese idols, Vienna china, Turkish rugs, and all the art lumber and fabricated rubbish of a bric–a–brac dealer's. It seemed a wonderful place to him; but, oh! was there one drop of water in it all? That was his single thought; for his tongue was parching, and

The Nurnberg Stove

his throat felt on fire, and his chest began to be dry and choked as with dust. There was not a drop of water, but there was a lattice window grated, and beyond the window was a wide stone ledge covered with snow. August cast one look at the locked door, darted out of his hiding-place, ran and opened the window, crammed the snow into his mouth again and again, and then flew back into the stove, drew the hay and straw over the place he entered by, tied the cords, and shut the brass door down on himself. He had brought some big icicles in with him, and by them his thirst was finally, if only temporarily, quenched. Then he sat still in the bottom of the stove, listening intently, wide awake, and once more recovering his natural boldness.

The thought of Dorothea kept nipping his heart and his conscience with a hard squeeze now and then; but he thought to himself, "If I can take her back Hirschvogel, then how pleased she will be, and how little 'Gilda will clap her hands!" He was not at all selfish in his love for Hirschvogel: he wanted it for them all at home quite as much as for himself. There was at the bottom of his mind a kind of ache of shame that his father—his own father—should have stripped their hearth and sold their honor thus.

A robin had been perched upon a stone griffin sculptured on a house-eave near. August had felt for the crumbs of his loaf in his pocket, and had thrown them to the little bird sitting so easily on the frozen snow.

In the darkness where he was he now heard a little song, made faint by the stove-wall and the window-glass that was between him and it, but still distinct and exquisitely sweet. It was the robin, singing after feeding on the crumbs. August, as he heard, burst into tears. He thought of Dorothea, who every morning threw out some grain or some bread on the snow before the church. "What use is it going there," she said, "if we forget the sweetest creatures God has made?" Poor Dorothea! Poor, good, tender, much-burdened little soul! He thought of her, till his tears ran like rain.

Yet it never once occurred to him to dream of going home. Hirschvogel was here.

VIII

PRESENTLY the key turned in the lock of the door, he heard heavy footsteps and the voice of the man who had said to his father, "You have a little mad dog; muzzle him!"

The Nurnberg Stove

The voice said, "Ay, ay, you have called me a fool many times. Now you shall see what I have gotten for two hundred dirty florins. Potztau-send! never did you do such a stroke of work."

Then the other voice grumbled and swore, and the steps of the two men approached more closely, and the heart of the child went pit-a-pat, pit-a-pat, as a mouse's does when it is on the top of a cheese and bears a housemaid's broom sweeping near. They began to strip the stove of its wrappings: that he could tell by the noise they made with the hay and the straw. Soon they had stripped it wholly: that, too, he knew by the oaths and exclamations of wonder and surprise and rapture which broke from the man who had not seen it before.

"A right royal thing! A wonderful and never-to-be-rivalled thing! Grander than the great stove of Hohen-Salzburg! Sublime! magnificent! matchless!"

So the epithets ran on in thick guttural voices, diffusing a smell of lager-beer so strong as they spoke that it reached August crouching in his stronghold. If they should open the door of the stove! That was his frantic fear. If they should open it, it would be all over with him. They would drag him out; most likely they would kill him, he thought, as his mother's young brother had been killed in the Wald.

The perspiration rolled off his forehead in his agony; but he had control enough over himself to keep quiet, and after standing by the Nurnberg master's work for nigh an hour, praising, marvelling, expatiating in the lengthy German tongue, the men moved to a little distance and began talking of sums of money and divided profits, of which discourse he could make out no meaning. All he could make out was that the name of the king—the king—the king came over very often in their arguments. He fancied at times they quarrelled, for they swore lustily and their voices rose hoarse and high; but after a while they seemed to pacify each other and agree to something, and were in great glee, and so in these merry spirits came and slapped the luminous sides of stately Hirschvogel, and shouted to it,—

"Old Mumchance, you have brought us rare good luck! To think you were smoking in a silly fool of a salt-baker's kitchen all these years!"

Then inside the stove August jumped up, with flaming cheeks and clinching hands, and was almost on the point of shouting out to them that they were the thieves and should say

The Nurnberg Stove

no evil of his father, when he remembered, just in time, that to breathe a word or make a sound was to bring ruin on himself and sever him forever from Hirschvogel. So he kept still, and the men barred the shutters of the little lattice and went out by the door, double-locking it after them. He had made out, from their talk that they were going to show Hirschvogel to some great person: therefore he kept quite still and dared not move.

Muffled sounds came to him through the shutters from the streets below,—the rolling of wheels, the clanging of church-bells, and bursts of that military music which is so seldom silent in the streets of Munich. An hour perhaps passed by; sounds of steps on the stairs kept him in perpetual apprehension. In the intensity of his anxiety, he forgot that he was hungry and many miles away from cheerful, Old World little Hall, lying by the clear gray river-water, with the ramparts of the mountains all around.

Presently the door opened again sharply. He could hear the two dealers' voices murmuring unctuous words, in which "honor," "gratitude," and many fine long noble titles played the chief parts. The voice of another person, more clear and refined than theirs, answered them curtly, and then, close by the Nurnberg stove and the boy's ear, ejaculated a single "Wunderschon!" August almost lost his terror for himself in his thrill of pride at his beloved Hirschvogel being thus admired in the great city. He thought the master-potter must be glad too.

"Wunderschon!" ejaculated the stranger a second time, and then examined the stove in all its parts, read all its mottoes, gazed long on all its devices.

"It must have been made for the Emperor Maximilian," he said at last; and the poor little boy, meanwhile, within, was "hugged up into nothing," as you children say, dreading that every moment he would open the stove. And open it truly he did, and examined the brass-work of the door; but inside it was so dark that crouching August passed unnoticed, screwed up into a ball like a hedgehog as he was. The gentleman shut to the door at length, without having seen anything strange inside it; and then he talked long and low with the tradesmen, and, as his accent was different from that which August was used to, the child could distinguish little that he said, except the name of the king and the word "gulden" again and again. After awhile he went away, one of the dealers accompanying him, one of them lingering behind to bar up the shutters. Then this one also withdrew again, double-locking the door.

The Nurnberg Stove

The poor little hedgehog uncurled itself and dared to breathe aloud.

What time was it?

Late in the day, he thought, for to accompany the stranger they had lighted a lamp; he had heard the scratch of the match, and through the brass fret-work had seen the lines of light.

He would have to pass the night here, that was certain. He and Hirschvogel were locked in, but at least they were together. If only he could have had something to eat! He thought with a pang of how at this hour at home they ate the sweet soup, sometimes with apples in it from Aunt Maila's farm orchard, and sang together, and listened to Dorothea's reading of little tales, and basked in the glow and delight that had beamed on them from the great Nurnberg fire-king.

"Oh, poor, poor little 'Gilda! What is she doing without the dear Hirschvogel?" he thought. Poor little 'Gilda! she had only now the black iron stove of the ugly little kitchen. Oh, how cruel of father!

August could not bear to hear the dealers blame or laugh at his father, but he did feel that it had been so, so cruel to sell Hirschvogel. The mere memory of all those long winter evenings, when they had all closed round it, and roasted chestnuts or crab-apples in it, and listened to the howling of the wind and the deep sound of the church-bells, and tried very much to make each other believe that the wolves still came down from the mountains into the streets of Hall, and were that very minute howling at the house-door,—all this memory coming on him with the sound of the city bells, and the knowledge that night drew near upon him so completely, being added to his hunger and his fear, so overcame him that he burst out crying for the fiftieth time since he had been inside the stove, and felt that he would starve to death, and wondered dreamily if Hirschvogel would care. Yes, he was sure Hirschvogel would care. Had he not decked it all summer long with Alpine roses and edelweiss and heaths and made it sweet with thyme and honeysuckle and great garden-lilies? Had he ever forgotten when Santa Claus came to make it its crown of holly and ivy and wreathe it all around?

"Oh, shelter me; save me; take care of me!" he prayed to the old fire-king, and forgot, poor little man, that he had come on this wild-goose chase northward to save and take

The Nurnberg Stove

care of Hirschvogel!

After a time he dropped asleep, as children can do when they weep, and little robust hill-born boys most surely do, be they where they may. It was not very cold in this lumber-room; it was tightly shut up, and very full of things, and at the back of it were the hot pipes of an adjacent house, where a great deal of fuel was burnt. Moreover, August's clothes were warm ones, and his blood was young. So he was not cold, though Munich is terribly cold in the nights of December; and he slept on and on,—which was a comfort to him, for he forgot his woes, and his perils, and his hunger, for a time.

IX

MIDNIGHT was once more chiming from all the brazen tongues of the city when he awoke, and, all being still around him, ventured to put his head out of the brass door of the stove to see why such a strange bright light was round him.

It was a very strange and brilliant light indeed; and yet, what is perhaps still stranger, it did not frighten or amaze him, nor did what he saw alarm him either, and yet I think it would have done you or me. For what he saw was nothing less than all the bric-a-brac in motion.

A big jug, an Apostel-Krug, of Kruessen, was solemnly dancing a minuet with a plump Faenza jar; a tall Dutch clock was going through a gavotte with a spindle-legged ancient chair; a very droll porcelain figure of Littenhausen was bowing to a very stiff soldier in terre cuite of Ulm; an old violin of Cremona was playing itself, and a queer little shrill plaintive music that thought itself merry came from a painted spinet covered with faded roses; some gilt Spanish leather had got up on the wall and laughed; a Dresden mirror was tripping about, crowned with flowers, and a Japanese bonze was riding along on a griffin; a slim Venetian rapier had come to blows with a stout Ferrara sabre, all about a little pale-faced chit of a damsel in white Nymphenburg china; and a portly Franconian pitcher in gres gris was calling aloud, "Oh, these Italians! always at feud!" But nobody listened to him at all. A great number of little Dresden cups and saucers were all skipping and waltzing; the teapots, with their broad round faces, were spinning their own lids like teetotums; the high-backed gilded chairs were having a game of cards together; and a little Saxe poodle, with a blue ribbon at its throat, was running from one to another,

The Nurnberg Stove

whilst a yellow cat of Cornelis Lachtleven's rode about on a Delft horse in blue pottery of 1489. Meanwhile the brilliant light shed on the scene came from three silver candelabra, though they had no candles set up in them; and, what is the greatest miracle of all, August looked on at these mad freaks and felt no sensation of wonder! He only, as he heard the violin and the spinet playing, felt an irresistible desire to dance too.

No doubt his face said what he wished; for a lovely little lady, all in pink and gold and white, with powdered hair, and high-heeled shoes, and all made of the very finest and fairest Meissen china, tripped up to him, and smiled, and gave him her hand, and led him out to a minuet. And he danced it perfectly,—poor little August in his thick, clumsy shoes, and his thick, clumsy sheepskin jacket, and his rough homespun linen, and his broad Tyrolean hat! He must have danced it perfectly; this dance of kings and queens in days when crowns were duly honored, for the lovely lady always smiled benignly and never scolded him at all, and danced so divinely herself to the stately measures the spinet was playing that August could not take his eyes off her till, their minuet ended, she sat down on her own white-and-gold bracket.

"I am the Princess of Saxe-Royale," she said to him, with a benignant smile; "and you have got through that minuet very fairly."

Then he ventured to say to her,—

"Madame my princess, could you tell me kindly why some of the figures and furniture dance and speak, and some lie up in a corner like lumber? It does make me curious. Is it rude to ask?"

For it greatly puzzled him why, when some of the bric-a-brac was all full of life and motion, some was quite still and had not a single thrill in it.

"My dear child," said the powdered lady, "is it possible that you do not know the reason? Why, those silent, dull things are imitation!"

This she said with so much decision that she evidently considered it a condensed but complete answer.

"Imitation?" repeated August, timidly, not understanding.

The Nurnberg Stove

"Of course! Lies, falsehoods, fabrications!" said the princess in pink shoes, very vivaciously. "They only pretend to be what we are! They never wake up: how can they? No imitation ever had any soul in it yet."

"Oh!" said August, humbly, not even sure that he understood entirely yet. He looked at Hirschvogel: surely it had a royal soul within it: would it not wake up and speak? Oh dear! how he longed to hear the voice of his fire-king! And he began to forget that he stood by a lady who sat upon a pedestal of gold-and-white china, with the year 1746 cut on it, and the Meissen mark.

"What will you be when you are a man?" said the little lady, sharply, for her black eyes were quick though her red lips were smiling. "Will you work for the Konigliche Porcellan-Manufactur, like my great dead Kandler?"

"I have never thought," said August, stammering; "at least—that is—I do wish—I do hope to be a painter, as was Master Augustin Hirschvogel at Nurnberg."

"Bravo!" said all the real bric-a-brac in one breath, and the two Italian rapiers left off fighting to cry, "Benone!"' For there is not a bit of true bric-a-brac in all Europe that does not know the names of the mighty masters.

August felt quite pleased to have won so much applause, and grew as red as the lady's shoes with bashful contentment.

"I knew all the Hirschvogel, from old Veit downwards," said a fat gres de Flandre beer-jug: "I myself was made at Nurnberg." And he bowed to the great stove very politely, taking off his own silver hat—I mean lid—with a courtly, sweep that he could scarcely have learned from burgomasters. The stove, however, was silent, and a sickening suspicion (for what is such heart-break as a suspicion of what we love?) came through the mind of August: Was Hirschvogel only imitation?

"No, no, no, no!" he said to himself, stoutly: though Hirschvogel never stirred, never spoke, yet would he keep all faith in it ! After all their happy years together, after all the nights of warmth and joy he owed it, should he doubt his own friend and hero, whose gilt lion's feet he had kissed in his babyhood? No, no, no, no!" he said, again, with so much emphasis that the Lady of Meissen looked sharply again at him.

The Nurnberg Stove

"So," she said, with pretty disdain; "no, believe me, they may pretend forever. They can never look like us! They imitate even our marks, but never can they look like the real thing, never, can they chassent de race."

"How should they?" said a bronze statuette of Vischer's. "They daub themselves green with verdigris, or sit out in the rain to get rusted; but green and rust are not patina; only the ages can give that!"

"And rep imitations are all in primary colors, staring colors, hot as the colors of a hostelry's sign-board!" said the Lady of Meissen, with a shiver.

"Well, there is a gres de Flandre over there, who pretends to be a Hans Kraut, as I am," said the jug with the silver hat, pointing with his handle to a jug that lay prone on its side in a corner. "He has copied me as exactly as it is given to moderns to copy us. Almost he might be mistaken for me. But yet what a difference there is ! How crude are his blues! how evidently done over the glaze are his black letters! He has tried to give himself my very twist; but what a lamentable exaggeration of that playful deviation in my lines which in his becomes actual deformity!"

"And look at that," said the gilt Cordovan leather, with a contemptuous glance at a broad piece of gilded leather spread out on a table. "They will sell him cheek by jowl with me, and give him my name; but look! I am overlaid with pure gold beaten thin as a film and laid on me in absolute honesty by worthy Diego de las Gorgias, worker in leather of lovely Cordova in the blessed reign of Ferdinand the Most Christian. His gilding is one part gold to eleven other parts of brass and rubbish, and it has been laid on him with a brush—a brush—pah! of course he will be as black as a crock in a few years' time, whist I am as bright as when I first was made, and, unless I am burnt as my Cordova burnt its heretics, I shall shine on forever."

"They carve pear-wood because it is so soft, and dye it brown, and call it me!" said an old oak cabinet, with a chuckle.

" That is not so painful; it does not vulgarize you so much as the cups they paint to-day and christen after me.'" said a Carl Theodor cup subdued in hue, yet gorgeous as a jewel.

The Nurnberg Stove

"Nothing can be so annoying as to see common gimcracks aping me!" interposed the princess in the pink shoes.

"They even steal my motto, though it is Scripture," said a Trauerkrug of Regensburg in black-and-white.

"And my own dots they put on plain English china creatures!" sighed the little white maid of Nymphenburg.

"And they sell hundreds and thousands of common china plates, calling them after me, and, baking my saints and my legends in a muffle of to-day; it is blasphemy!" said a stout plate of Gubbio, which in its year of birth had seen the face of Maestro Giorgio.

"That is what is so terrible in these bric-a-brac places," said the princess of Meissen. "It brings one in contact with such low, imitative creatures; one really is safe nowhere nowadays unless under glass at the Louvre or South Kensington."

"And they get even there," sighed the gres de Flandre. "A terrible thing happened to a dear friend of mine, a terre cuite of Blasius (you know the terres cuites of Blasius date from 1560). Well, he was put under glass in a museum that shall be nameless, and he found himself set next to his own imitation born and baked yesterday at Frankfort, and what think you the miserable creature said to him, with a grin? Old Pipe-clay,—that is what he called my friend,—the fellow that bought me got just as much commission on me as the fellow that bought you, and that was all that he thought about. You know it is only the public money that goes!' And the horrid creature grinned again till he actually cracked himself. There is a Providence above all things, even museums."

"Providence might have interfered before, and saved the public money," said the little Meissen lady with the pink shoes.

"After all, does it matter?" said a Dutch jar of Haarlem. "All the shamming in the world will not make them us!"

"One does not like to be vulgarized," said the Lady of Meissen, angrily.

The Nurnberg Stove

"My maker, the Krabbetje," [Jan Asselyn, called Krabbetje, the Little Crab, born 1610, master-potter of Delft and Haarlem.] did not trouble his head about that," said the Haarlem jar, proudly. "The Krabbetje made me for the kitchen, the bright, clean, snow-white Dutch kitchen, wellnigh three centuries ago, and now I am thought worthy the palace; yet I wish I were at home; yes, I wish I could see the good, Dutch vrouw, and the shining canals, and the great green meadows dotted with the kine."

"Ah! if we could all go back to our makers!" sighed the Gubbio plate, thinking of Giorgio Andreoli and the glad and gracious days of the Renaissance: and somehow the words touched the frolicsome souls of the dancing jars, the spinning teapots, the chairs that were playing cards; and the violin stopped its merry music with a sob, and the spinet sighed,—thinking of dead hands.

Even the little Saxe poodle howled for a master forever lost; and only the swords went on quarrelling, and made such a clattering noise that the Japanese bonze rode at them on his monster and knocked them both right over, and they lay straight and still, looking foolish, and the little Nymphenburg maid, though she was crying, smiled and almost laughed.

Then from where the great stove stood there came a solemn voice.

All eyes turned upon Hirschvogel, and the heart of its little human comrade gave a great jump of joy.

"My friends," said that clear voice from the turret of Nurnberg faience, "I have listened to all you have said. There is too much talking among the Mortalities whom one of themselves has called the Windbags. Let not us be like them. I hear among men so much vain speech, so much precious breath and precious time wasted in empty boasts, foolish anger, useless reiteration, blatant argument, ignoble mouthings, that I have learned to deem speech a curse, laid on man to weaken and envenom all his undertakings. For over two hundred years I have never spoken myself: you, I hear, are not so reticent. I only speak now because one of you said a beautiful thing that touched me. If we all might but go back to our makers! Ah, yes! if we might! We were made in days when even men were true creatures, and so we, the work of their hands, were true too. We, the begotten of ancient days, derive all the value in us from the fact that our makers wrought at us with zeal, with piety, with integrity, with faith,—not to win fortunes or to glut a market, but to do nobly an honest thing and create for the honor of the Arts and God. I see amidst you a

The Nurnberg Stove

little human thing who loves me, and in his own ignorant childish way loves it. Now, I want him forever to remember this night and these words; to remember that we are what we are, and precious in the eyes of the world, because centuries ago those who were of single mind and of pure hand so created us, scorning sham and haste and counterfeit. Well do I recollect my master, Augustin Hirschvogel. He led a wise and blameless life, and wrought in loyalty and love, and made his time beautiful thereby, like one of his own rich, many-colored church casements, that told holy tales as the sun streamed through them. Ah, yes, my friends, to go back to our masters!—that would be the best that could befall us. But they are gone, and even the perishable labors of their lives outlive them. For many, many years I, once honored of emperors, dwelt in a humble house and warmed in successive winters three generations of little, cold, hungry children. When I warmed them they forgot that they were hungry; they laughed and told tales, and slept at last about my feet. Then I knew that humble as had become my lot it was one that my master would have wished for me, and I was content. Sometimes a tired woman would creep up to me, and smile because she was near me, and point out my golden crown or my, ruddy fruit to a baby in her arms. That was better than to stand in a great hall of a great city, cold and empty, even though wise men came to gaze and throngs of fools gaped, passing with flattering words. Where I go now I know not; but since I go from that humble house where they loved me, I shall be sad and alone. They pass so soon,—those fleeting mortal lives! Only we endure,—we, the things that the human brain creates. We can but bless them a little as they glide by: if we have done that, we have done what our masters wished. So in us our masters, being dead, yet may speak and live."

Then the voice sank away in silence, and a strange golden light that had shone on the great stove faded away; so also the light died down in the silver candelabra. A soft, pathetic melody stole gently through the room. It came from the old, old spinet that was covered with the faded roses.

Then that sad, sighing music of a by gone day died too; the clocks of the city struck six of the morning; day was rising over the Bayerischenwald. August awoke with a great start, and found himself lying on the bare bricks of the floor of the chamber, and all the bric-a-brac was lying quite still all around. The pretty Lady of Meissen was motionless on her porcelain bracket, and the little Saxe poodle was quiet at her side.

He rose slowly to his feet. He was very cold, but he was not sensible of it or of the hunger that was gnawing his little empty entrails. He was absorbed in the wondrous sight, in the wondrous sounds, that he had seen and heard.

X

ALL was dark around him. Was it still midnight or had morning come? Morning, surely; for against the barred shutters he heard the tiny song of the robin.

Tramp, tramp, too, came a heavy step up the stair. He had but a moment in which to scramble back into the interior of the great stove, when the door opened and the two dealers entered, bringing burning candles with them to see their way.

August was scarcely conscious of danger more than he was of cold or hunger. A marvellous sense of courage, of security, of happiness, was about him, like strong and gentle arms enfolding him and lifting him upwards—upwards—upwards! Hirschvogel would defend him.

The dealers undid the shutters, scaring the red-breast away, and then tramped about in their heavy boots and chattered in contented voices, and began to wrap up the stove once more in all its straw and hay and cordage.

It never once occurred to them to glance inside. Why should they look inside a stove that they had bought and were about to sell again for all its glorious beauty of exterior?

The child still did not feel afraid. A great exaltation had come to him: he was like one lifted up by his angels.

Presently the two traders called up their porters, and the stove, heedfully swathed and wrapped and tended as though it were some sick prince going on a journey, was borne on the shoulders of six stout Bavarians down the stairs and out of the door into the Marienplatz. Even behind all those wrappings August felt the icy bite of the intense cold of the outer air at dawn of a winter's day in Munich. The men moved the stove with exceeding gentleness and care, so that he had often been far more roughly shaken in his big brothers' arms than he was in his journey now; and though both hunger and thirst made themselves felt, being foes that will take no denial, he was still in that state of nervous exaltation which deadens all physical suffering and is at once a cordial and an

The Nurnberg Stove

opiate. He had heard Hirschvogel speak; that was enough.

The stout carriers tramped through the city, six of them, with the Nurnberg fire-castle on their brawny shoulders, and went right across Munich to the railway-station, and August in the dark recognized all the ugly, jangling, pounding, roaring, hissing railway-noises, and thought, despite his courage and excitement, "Will it be a very long journey?" For his stomach had at times an odd sinking sensation, and his head sadly often felt light and swimming. If it was a very, very long journey he felt half afraid that he would be dead or something bad before the end, and Hirschvogel would be so lonely: that was what he thought most about; not much about himself, and not much about Dorothea and the house at home. He was "high strung to high emprise," and could not look behind him.

Whether for a long or a short journey, whether for weal or woe, the stove with August still within it was once more hoisted up into a great van; but this time it was not all alone, and the two dealers as well as the six porters were all with it.

He in his darkness knew that; for he heard their voices. The train glided away over the Bavarian plain southward; and he heard the men say something of Berg and the Wurm-See, but their German was strange to him, and he could not make out what these names meant.

The train rolled on, with all its fume and fuss, and roar of steam, and stench of oil and burning coal. It had to go quietly and slowly on account of the snow which was falling, and which had fallen all night.

"He might have waited till he came to the city," grumbled one man to another. "What weather to stay on at Berg!"

But who he was that stayed on at Berg, August could not make out at all.

Though the men grumbled about the state of the roads and the season, they were hilarious and well content, for they laughed often, and, when they swore, did so good-humoredly, and promised their porters fine presents at New-Year; and August, like a shrewd little boy as he was, who even in the secluded Innthal had learned that money is the chief mover of men's mirth, thought to himself, with a terrible pang,—

The Nurnberg Stove

"They have sold Hirschvogel for some great sum. They have sold him already!"

Then his heart grew faint and sick within him, for he knew very well that he must soon die, shut up without food and water thus; and what new owner of the great fire-palace would ever permit him to dwell in it?

"Never mind; I will die," thought he; "and Hirschvogel will know it."

Perhaps you think him a very foolish little fellow; but I do not.

It is always good to be loyal and ready to endure to the end.

It is but an hour and a quarter that the train usually takes to pass from Munich to the Wurm-See or Lake of Starnberg; but this morning the journey was much slower, because the way was encumbered by snow. When it did reach Possenhofen and stop, and the Nurnberg stove was lifted out once more, August could see through the fret-work of the brass door, as the stove stood upright facing the lake, that this Wurm-See was a calm and noble piece of water, of great width, with low wooded banks and distant mountains, a peaceful, serene place, full of rest.

It was now near ten o'clock. The sun had come forth; there was a clear gray sky here-abouts; the snow was not falling, though it lay white and smooth everywhere, down to the edge of the water, which before long would itself be ice.

Before he had time to get more than a glimpse of the green gliding surface, the stove was again lifted up and placed on a large boat that was in waiting,—one of those very long and huge boats which the women in these parts use as laundries, and the men as timber-rafts. The stove, with much labor and much expenditure of time and care, was hoisted into this, and August would have grown sick and giddy with the heaving and falling if his big brothers had not long used him to such tossing about, so that he was as much at ease head, as feet, downward. The stove once in it safely with its guardians, the big boat moved across the lake to Leoni. How a little hamlet on a Bavarian lake got that Tuscan-sounding name I cannot tell; but Leoni it is. The big boat was a long time crossing: the lake here is about three miles broad, and these heavy barges are unwieldy and heavy to move, even though they are towed and tugged at from the shore.

The Nurnberg Stove

"If we should be too late !" the two dealers muttered to each other, in agitation and alarm. "He said eleven o'clock."

"Who was he?" thought August; "the buyer, of course, of Hirschvogel." The slow passage across the Wurm–See was accomplished at length: the lake was placid; there was a sweet calm in the air and on the water; there was a great deal of snow in the sky, though the sun was shining and gave a solemn hush to the atmosphere. Boats and one little steamer were going up and down; in the clear frosty light the distant mountains of Zillerthal and the Algau Alps were visible; market–people, cloaked and furred, went by on the water or on the banks; the deep woods of the shores were black and gray and brown. Poor August could see nothing of a scene that would have delighted him; as the stove was now set, he could only see the old worm–eaten wood of the huge barge.

Presently they touched the pier at Leoni.

"Now, men, for a stout mile and half! You shall drink your reward at Christmas–time," said one of the dealers to his porters, who, stout, strong men as they were, showed a disposition to grumble at their task. Encouraged by large promises, they shouldered sullenly the Nurnberg stove, grumbling again at its preposterous weight, but little dreaming that they carried within it a small, panting, trembling boy, for, August began to tremble now that he was about to see the future owner of Hirschvogel.

"If he look a good, kind man," he thought, "I will beg him to let me stay with it."

XI

THE porters began their toilsome journey, and moved off from the village pier. He could see nothing, for the brass door was over his head, and all that gleamed through it was the clear gray sky. He had been tilted on to his back, and if he had not been a little mountaineer, used to hanging head–downwards over crevasses, and, moreover, seasoned to rough treatment by the hunters and guides of the hills and the salt–workers in the town, he would have been made ill and sick by the bruising and shaking and many changes of position to which he had been subjected.

The way the men took was a mile and a half in length, but the road was heavy with snow,

The Nurnberg Stove

and the burden they bore was heavier still. The dealers cheered them on, swore at them and praised them in one breath; besought them and reiterated their splendid promises, for a clock was striking eleven, and they had been ordered to reach their destination at that hour, and, though the air was so cold, the heat-drops rolled off their foreheads as they walked, they were so frightened at being late. But the porters would not budge a foot quicker than they chose, and as they were not poor four-footed carriers their employers dared not thrash them, though most willingly would they have done so.

The road seemed terribly long to the anxious tradesmen, to the plodding porters, to the poor little man inside the stove, as be kept sinking and rising, sinking and rising, with each of their steps.

Where they were going he had no idea, only, after a very long time he lost the sense of the fresh icy wind blowing on his face through the brasswork above, and felt by their movements beneath him that they were mounting steps or stairs. Then he heard a great many different voices, but he could not understand what was being said. He felt that his bearers paused some time, then moved on and on again. Their feet went so softly he thought they must be moving on carpet, and as he felt a warm air come to him he concluded that he was in some heated chambers, for he was a clever little fellow, and could put two and two together, though he was so hungry and so thirsty and his empty stomach felt so strangely. They must have gone, be thought, through some very great number of rooms, for they walked so long on and on, on and on. At last the stove was set down again, and, happily for him, set so that his feet were downward.

What he fancied was that he was in some museum, like that which he had seen in the city of Innspruck.

The voices he heard were very hushed, and the steps seemed to go away, far away, leaving him alone with Hirschvogel. He dared not look out, but he peeped through the brass work, and all he could see was a big carved lion's head in ivory, with a gold crown atop. It belonged to a velvet fauteuil, but he could not see the chair, only the ivory lion.

There was a delicious fragrance in the air,—a fragrance as of flowers. "Only how can it be flowers?" thought August. "It is December!"

The Nurnberg Stove

From afar off, as it seemed, there came a dreamy, exquisite music, as sweet as the spinet's had been, but so much fuller, so much richer, seeming as though a chorus of angels were singing all together. August ceased to think of the museum: he thought of heaven. "Are we gone to the Master?" he thought, remembering the words of Hirschvogel.

All was so still around him; there was no sound anywhere except the sound of the far-off choral music.

He did not know it, but he was in the royal castle of Berg, and the music he heard was the music of Wagner, who was playing in a distant room some of the motives of "Parsival."

Presently he heard a fresh step near him, and he heard a low voice say, close behind him, "So!" An exclamation no doubt, be thought, of admiration and wonder at the beauty of Hirschvogel.

Then the same voice said, after a long pause, during which no doubt, as August thought, this new-comer was examining all the details of the wondrous fire-tower, "It was well bought; it is exceedingly beautiful! It is most undoubtedly the work of Augustin Hirschvogel."

Then the hand of the speaker turned the round handle of the brass door, and the fainting soul of the poor little prisoner within grew sick with fear.

The handle turned, the door was slowly drawn open, some one bent down and looked in, and the same voice that he had heard in praise of its beauty called aloud, in surprise, "What is this in it? A live child!"

Then August, terrified beyond all self-control, and dominated by one master-passion, sprang out of the body of the stove and fell at the feet of the speaker

"Oh, let me stay! Pray, meinherr, let me stay!" he sobbed. "I have come all the way with Hirschvogel!"

Some gentlemen's hands seized him, not gently by any means, and their lips angrily muttered in his ear, "Little knave, peace! be quiet! hold your tongue! It is the king!"

The Nurnberg Stove

They were about to drag him out of the august atmosphere as if he had been some venomous, dangerous beast come there to slay, but the voice he had heard speak of the stove said, in kind accents, "Poor little child! he is very young. Let him go: let him speak to me."

The word of a king is law to his courtiers: so, sorely against their wish, the angry and astonished chamberlains let August slide out of their grasp, and he stood there in his little rough sheepskin coat and his thick, mud-covered boots, with his curling hair all in a tangle, in the midst of the most beautiful chamber he had ever dreamed of, and in the presence of a young man with a beautiful dark face, and eyes full of dreams and fire; and the young man said to him,—

"My child, how came you here, hidden in this stove? Be not afraid: tell me the truth. I am the king."

August in an instinct of homage cast his great battered black hat with the tarnished gold tassels down on the floor of the room, and folded his little brown hands in supplication. He was too intensely in earnest to be in any way abashed; he was too lifted out of himself by his love for Hirschvogel to be conscious of any awe before any earthly majesty. He was only so glad—so glad it was the king. Kings were always kind; so the Tyrolese think, who love their lords.

"Oh, dear king!" he said, with trembling entreaty in his faint little voice, "Hirschvogel was ours, and we have loved it all our lives; and father sold it. And when I saw that it did really go from us, then I said to myself I would go with it; and I have come all the way inside it. And last night it spoke and said beautiful things. And I do pray you to let me live with it, and I will go out every morning and cut wood for it and you, if only you will let me stay beside it. No one ever has fed it with fuel but me since I grew big enough, and it loves me;—it does indeed; it said so last night; and it said that it had been happier with us than if it were in any palace—"

And then his breath failed him, and, as he lifted his little, eager, pale face to the young king's, great tears were falling down his cheeks.

Now, the king likes all poetic and uncommon things, and there was that in the child's face which pleased and touched him. He motioned to his gentlemen to leave the little boy

The Nurnberg Stove

alone.

"What is your name?" he asked him.

"I am August Strehla. My father is Karl Strehla. We live in Hall, in the Innthal; and Hirschvogel has been ours so long,—so long!"

His lips quivered with a broken sob.

"And have you truly travelled inside this stove all the way from Tyrol?"

"Yes," said August; "no one thought to look inside till you did."

The king laughed; then another view of the matter occurred to him.

"Who bought the stove of your father?" he inquired.

"Traders of Munich," said August, who did not know that he ought not to have spoken to the king as to a simple citizen, and whose little brain was whirling and spinning dizzily round its one central idea.

"What sum did they pay your father, do you know?" asked the sovereign.

"Two hundred florins," said August, with a great sigh of shame. "It was so much money, and he is so poor, and there are so many of us."

The king turned to his gentlemen-in-waiting. "Did these dealers of Munich come with the stove."

He was answered in the affirmative. He desired them to be sought for and brought before him. As one of his chamberlains hastened on the errand, the monarch looked at August with compassion.

"You are very pale, little fellow: when did you eat last?"

"I had some bread and sausage with me; yesterday afternoon I finished it."

The Nurnberg Stove

"You would like to eat now?"

"If I might have a little water I would be glad; my throat is very dry."

The king had water and wine brought for him, and cake also; but August, though he drank eagerly, could not swallow anything. His mind was in too great a tumult.

"May I stay with Hirschvogel?—may I stay?" he said, with feverish agitation.

"Wait a little," said the king, and asked, abruptly, "What do you wish to be when you are a man?"

"A painter. I wish to be what Hirschvogel was,—I mean the master that made my Hirschvogel."

"I understand," said the king.

Then the two dealers were brought into their sovereign's presence. They were so terribly alarmed, not being either so innocent or so ignorant as August was, that they were trembling as though they were being led to the slaughter, and they were so utterly astonished too at a child having come all the way from Tyrol in the stove, as a gentleman of the court had just told them this child had done, that they could not tell what to say or where to look, and presented a very foolish aspect indeed.

"Did you buy this Nurnberg stove of this little boy's father for two hundred florins?" the king asked them; and his voice was no longer soft and kind as it had been when addressing the child, but very stern.

"Yes, your majesty," murmured the trembling traders.

"And how much did the gentleman who purchased it for me give to you?"

"Two thousand ducats, your majesty," muttered the dealers, frightened out of their wits, and telling the truth in their fright.

The Nurnberg Stove

The gentleman was not present: he was a trusted counsellor in art matters of the king's, and often made purchases for him.

The king smiled a little, and said nothing. The gentleman had made out the price to him as eleven thousand ducats.

"You will give at once to this boy's father the two thousand gold ducats that you received, less the two hundred Austrian florins that you paid him," said the king to his humiliated and abject subjects. "You are great rogues. Be thankful you are not more greatly punished."

He dismissed them by a sign to his courtiers, and to one of these gave the mission of making the dealers of the Marienplatz disgorge their ill-gotten gains.

August heard, and felt dazzled yet miserable. Two thousand gold Bavarian ducats for his father! Why, his father would never need to go any more to the salt-baking! And yet, whether for ducats or for florins, Hirschvogel was sold just the same, and would the king let him stay with it?—would he?

"Oh, do! oh, please do!" he murmured, joining his little brown weather-stained hands, and kneeling down before the young monarch, who himself stood absorbed in painful thought, for the deception so basely practised for the greedy sake of gain on him by a trusted counsellor was bitter to him.

He looked down on the child, and as he did so smiled once more.

"Rise up, my little man," he said, in a kind voice; "kneel only to your God. Will I let you stay with your Hirschvogel? Yes, I will; you shall stay at my court, and you shall be taught to be a painter,—in oils or on porcelain as you will, and you must grow up worthily, and win all the laurels at our Schools of Art, and if when you are twenty-one years old you have done well and bravely, then I will give you your Nurnberg stove, or, if I am no more living, then those who reign after me shall do so. And now go away with this gentleman, and be not afraid, and you shall light a fire every morning in Hirschvogel, but you will not need to go out and cut the wood."

The Nurnberg Stove

Then he smiled and stretched out his hand; the courtiers tried to make August understand that he ought to bow and touch it with his lips, but August could not understand that anyhow; he was too happy. He threw his two arms about the king's knees, and kissed his feet passionately; then he lost all sense of where he was, and fainted away from hunger, and tire, and emotion, and wondrous joy.

As the darkness of his swoon closed in on him, he heard in his fancy the voice from Hirschvogel saying,—

"Let us be worthy our maker!"

He is only a scholar yet, but he is a happy scholar, and promises to be a great man. Sometimes he goes back for a few days to Hall, where the gold ducats have made his father prosperous. In the old house-room there is a large white porcelain stove of Munich, the king's gift to Dorothea and 'Gilda.

And August never goes home without going into the great church and saying his thanks to God, who blessed his strange winter's journey in the Nurnberg stove. As for his dream in the dealers' room that night, he will never admit that he did dream it; he still declares that he saw it all, and heard the voice of Hirschvogel. And who shall say that he did not? for what is the gift of the poet and the artist except to see the sights which others cannot see and to hear the sounds that others cannot hear?

CPSIA information can be obtained at www.ICGtesting.com
Printed in the USA
LVOW11*1915051113

360104LV00041B/525/P